A Gift For:

From:

Copyright © 2019 Hallmark Licensing, LLC

Published by Hallmark Gift Books,
a division of Hallmark Cards, Inc.,
Kansas City, MO 64141
Visit us online at Hallmark.com.

Editorial Director: Delia Berrigan
Editor: Kara Goodier
Designer: Brian Pilachowski
Production Designer: Dan Horton

ISBN: 978-1-63059-600-2
KCX1021

Made in China
0620

There's Snow More Room!

The Flurry of the Frostbottom Family Photo

Hallmark

A STORY FROM THE HALLMARK HOLIDAY SERIES
Written by Joey Benevento   Illustrated by Mike Esberg

In Flurryburg, city of snowdrifts,
where the icebergs are something to see,
the cheer-loving Frostbottom family
had just finished trimming their tree.

"Well, snicker my doodles!" Dad marveled.
"That's almost too pretty to bear!
Now Snoseph, stand next to your mama,
and I'll take a picture to share."

But Snoseph said, "What about you, Dad?
The whole family should be in the pic!
We can capture the memory forever—
let's all take a selfie real quick!"

When they sat on the couch, their dog Nutmeg
hopped up, with an "Arf! Arf! Arooooo!"
"Oh, Nutmeg, come join us!" said Mama.
"You're part of the family, too."

But before they could take any pictures,
they heard their front doorbell's clear chime.
It was Snoseph's best friend, little Snophie,
who said, "Hey, guys! Is this a bad time?"

"We're taking a family photo!"
Snoseph said, giving Snophie a grin.
"And I think that my very best buddy
should be in it, so please, come on in!"

"Come on in?" said Ms. Blizzard, the neighbor,
who suddenly burst from the mist.
"You're taking a picture? How lovely!
I'll join—if you really insist!"

Then the mailman arrived, and the trash man.

Ms. Blizzard got very excited.

"We're taking a picture," she told them.

"Spread the word. Everybody's invited!"

"Um, Son?" Mama asked in a whisper,
"how many can one selfie fit?"
"Not sure," he replied, "but don't worry.
We'll just have to squeeze in a bit."

Things started to snowball like crazy!
First the grocer walked in, then the baker,
then cashiers, engineers, the town juggler,
and a second-rate flügelhorn-maker!

By this point, the Frostbottom cottage

was just about ready to burst.

"Picture time?" Mama asked. Snoseph answered:

"Let me pick a good angle out first."

But whether he hung from the rafters

(while their friends all packed in like sardines)

or stood on the stairs, chairs, or tables,

he could not fit them all on his screen.

"Perhaps I can help," said the mailman,
who pushed through the circle to speak,
"I'm here to deliver a package.
You might want to give it a peek."

He handed the package to Snoseph,
and Snophie said, "Open it, quick!"
He did, and inside was a shiny,
brand-new, extra-long selfie stick!

Extra-long, but it had to be longer!
Snoseph borrowed a thing (or eighteen)
from his guests, and created the longest
selfie-stick that the world's ever seen!

So the Frostbottom family picture
was certainly one of a kind.
It was bigger than they had expected,
and more crowded, but they didn't mind.

For whether you live in the tundra
or in Flurryburg, where it's all frozen,
your family's not just who you live with—
it's all the good people you've chosen.

THE FROSTBOTTOM FAMILY and Friends!

If this chilly adventure warmed your heart,
or if perhaps you just liked the art,
we would love to hear from you.

Please write a review at Hallmark.com,
e-mail us at booknotes@hallmark.com,
or send your comments to:

Hallmark Book Feedback
P.O. Box 419034
Mail Drop 100
Kansas City, MO 64141

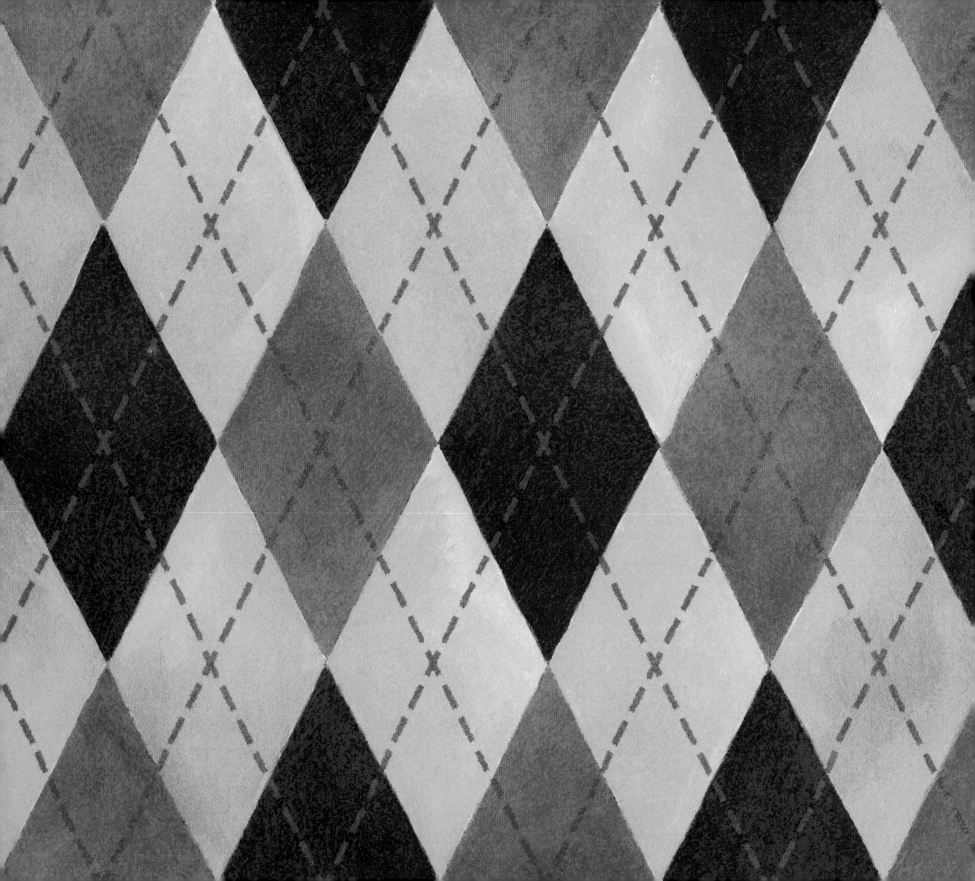